The CAT
that Walked by Himself

For Jack Tom and...

Find out more about

Rudyard Kipling's
JUST so STORIES

at Shoo Rayner's fabulous website,

www.shoo-rayner.co.uk

First published in 2007 by Orchard Books
First paperback publication in 2008

ORCHARD BOOKS
338 Euston Road, London NW1 3BH
Orchard Books Australia
Level 17/207 Kent St, Sydney, NSW 2000

ISBN 978 1 84616 405 7 (hardback)
ISBN 978 1 84616 413 2 (paperback)

A CIP catalogue record for this book is available from the British Library.

1 3 5 7 9 10 8 6 4 2 (hardback)
1 3 5 7 9 10 8 6 4 2 (paperback)

Printed in England by Antony Rowe Ltd, Chippenham, Wiltshire

Orchard Books is a division of Hachette Children's Books,
an Hachette Livre UK company.

www.orchardbooks.co.uk

Rudyard Kipling's
JUST SO STORIES

The CAT
that Walked by Himself

Retold and illustrated by
SHOO RAYNER

ORCHARD BOOKS

Long, long ago, at the very beginning of time, when all the animals were still as wild as can be, the wildest of all the wild animals was the Cat.

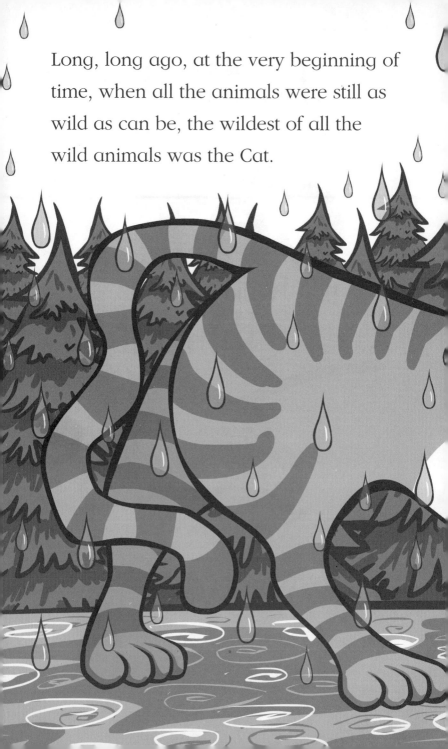

He walked by himself in the Wet Wild Woods, waving his wild tail and walking by his wild lone self, and all places were alike to him.

Man was dreadfully wild too. He was only tamed when he met a Woman, who found a nice dry Cave, instead of a heap of wet leaves.

There she lit a fire at the back of the Cave and she said, "Wipe your feet when you come in, dear, and now we'll keep house."

Keeping House in a Nice Dry Cave

The most important thing is to keep out the cold. To do this, make a curtain from animal skins and hang it in the mouth of the cave.

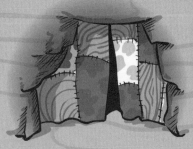

Then make a nice, warm fire to heat the cave and dry it out.

Soon, the Dog came in from the wild and became their friend.

The Woman
let him eat
bones,

as long as he kept
guard and helped
the Man to hunt.

Then the Horse and the Cow became their servants.

The Woman
let the Horse
eat sweet hay,
if the Man
could ride him,

and let the Cow
eat grass, if she
gave them milk
every day.

The Cat watched from outside. "This woman is clever," he said to himself, "but I am the Cat who walks by himself, and all places are alike to me."

One day the Cat saw the Woman
milking the Cow, and he saw the
light of the fire in the Cave, and he
smelt the smell of warm, white milk.

"Wild Thing," the Woman
said, "go back to the Wet
Wild Woods. We don't need
any more friends or servants."

"I am not a friend," said the Cat, "nor a servant. I am the Cat who walks by himself, and I wish to come into your Cave."

The Woman laughed. "If you are the Cat who walks by himself, and all places are alike to you, go away and walk by yourself in all your likely places."

14

The Cat
looked sorry.

"Can't I ever come
into the Cave and sit by
the warm fire and drink
the warm, white milk?"
he asked. "You are very
wise and beautiful. You
shouldn't be cruel – not
even to a Cat."

15

"I know I'm wise," said the Woman, "but I did not know I was beautiful. I will make a bargain with you. If ever I say one word in your praise, you can come into the Cave."

"And if you say two words in my praise?" said the Cat.

"I won't," said the
Woman, "but if I do,
you may sit by the
fire in the Cave."
"And if you say
three words?" said
the Cat.

"I never shall," said the Woman, "but
if I do, you may drink warm, white milk
three times a day for always and
always and always."

17

The Cat arched his back
and said, "Let the Curtain at
the mouth of the Cave, and
the Fire at the back of the
Cave, and the Milk-pots that
stand beside the Fire,
remember this bargain."

Then the Cat went away through the
Wet Wild Woods waving his wild tail
and walking by his wild lone self.

The Wet Wild Woods

The wet, wild woods are very wet and very wild.

BEWARE!

After a while, the Woman forgot all about him. Only the little upside-down Bat, that hung inside the Cave, knew where the Cat hid. Every evening he would fly to the Cat with news.

One evening the Bat said, "There is a Baby in the Cave. He is new and pink and fat and small, and the Woman is very fond of him."

"Ah," said the Cat, listening, "and what is the Baby fond of?"

"He likes things that are soft and tickly," said the Bat. "He likes to hold warm things in his arms when he goes to sleep, and he likes being played with."

"Ah," said the Cat, listening. "My time has come."

21

The next day, the Woman was busy cooking, but the Baby cried and cried. She carried the Baby outside and gave him a handful of pebbles to play with. But still the Baby cried.

The Cat put out his
paddy paw and patted
the Baby on the cheek,
and it cooed.

The Cat rubbed
against the Baby's
fat knees and tickled
it under its fat chin
with his tail.

The Baby laughed.
The Woman heard
him and smiled.

Then the little
upside-down Bat
said to the Woman,
"a Wild Thing from
the Wild Woods
is playing with
your Baby."

"A blessing on that Wild Thing, whoever he may be," said the Woman, straightening her back. "He's made the Baby happy and let me get on."

That very second, the Curtain that was stretched across the mouth of the Cave fell down – whoosh!

It remembered the bargain the
Woman had made with the Cat.
When the Woman picked up the
Curtain, lo and behold –

the Cat was
sitting quite
comfy inside
the Cave!

The Cat smiled, "It is I! You spoke a word in my praise. Now I can sit in the Cave for always and always and always.

But still I am the Cat who walks by himself, and all places are alike to me."

The Woman was very angry. She shut her lips tight and took up her spinning-wheel and began to spin.

But the Baby cried
and cried because
the Cat had gone
away. The Woman
could not calm him.

"Drag some thread along
the floor," said the Cat, "and
I will make your Baby laugh
as loud as he is crying now."

"I will," said the Woman, "because I am at my wits' end, but I'll not thank you for it."

The Cat chased the thread and patted it with his paws

and rolled head over heels, and pretended to lose it,

and pounced down
upon it again,

till the Baby laughed
as loudly as it had been
crying, till it grew tired
and settled down with
the Cat in its arms.

33

The Cat purred, loud and low, low and loud, till the Baby fell fast asleep. The Woman smiled and said, "That was wonderfully done. Without doubt, you are a very clever Cat."

That very second, the smoke of the Fire at the back of the Cave came down in clouds from the roof – puff!

It remembered the bargain the Woman had made with the Cat. When the smoke cleared away, lo and behold – the Cat was sitting quite comfy next to the Fire!

The Cat smiled, "It is I! You spoke a second word in my praise, and now I can sit by the warm Fire at the back of the Cave for always and always and always.

But still I am the Cat who walks by himself, and all places are alike to me."

How to Make a Fire

Make sure that whatever
you use is very dry.

Rub two sticks
together.

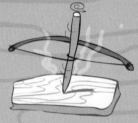

Use a bow to spin
a stick on some
dry wood.

Make sparks with
iron and flint.

Get a tree hit by
a lightning bolt.

The Woman was so angry. She shut her lips tight. The Cave became so still that a wee, little Mouse crept out of a corner and ran across the floor.

"Eeeeek!" the Woman screamed as she jumped up on the footstool in front of the fire.

In one jump, the Cat caught the little Mouse. The Woman said, "A hundred thanks. No one is quick enough to catch little Mice like that. You must be very wise."

That very second, the Milk-pot that stood by the fire cracked in two pieces – ffft! It remembered the bargain she had made with the Cat.

40

Very Quick Animals

The cheetah is the fastest land animal
at 70 m.p.h. (miles per hour).

The chameleon has the fastest tongue.

Racing pigeons can
fly at 100 m.p.h.!

The sailfish can
swim at 68 m.p.h.

When the Woman jumped down from the footstool, lo and behold – the Cat was lapping up the warm, white milk that had spilled on the floor.

The Cat smiled, "It is I! You spoke a third word in my praise, and now I can drink the warm, white milk three times a day for always and always and always. But still I am the Cat who walks by himself, and all places are alike to me."

Then the Woman
laughed and gave the Cat
a bowl of the warm, white
milk. "You are very, very
clever," she told him.

From that day to this, the Cat
keeps his side of the bargain.

He catches Mice, and is kind to
Babies when he is in the house, just
as long as they do not pull his tail
too hard.

But when he has done that, and between times, and when the moon gets up and night comes, he is still the Cat that walks by himself, and all places are alike to him.

Then he goes
out to the Wet
Wild Woods

or up the Wet
Wild Trees

or onto the Wet Wild
Roofs, waving his
wild tail and walking
by his wild lone self.

Rudyard Kipling's JUST SO STORIES

Retold and illustrated by

SHOO RAYNER

All priced at £8.99

Rudyard Kipling's Just So Stories are available from all good bookshops,
or can be ordered direct from
the publisher: Orchard Books, PO BOX 29, Douglas IM99 1BQ
Credit card orders please telephone 01624 836000
or fax 01624 837033 or visit our internet site: www.orchardbooks.co.uk
or e-mail: bookshop@enterprise.net for details.

To order please quote title, author and ISBN
and your full name and address.
Cheques and postal orders should be made payable to 'Bookpost plc.'
Postage and packing is FREE within the UK
(overseas customers should add £2.00 per book).

Prices and availability are subject to change.